MY NAME

# María Isabel

by Alma Flor Ada

*illustrated by* K. Dyble Thompson

*translated from the Spanish by* Ana M. Cerro

SCHOLASTIC INC.

New York   Toronto   London   Auckland   Sydney

Text copyright © 1993 by Alma Flor Ada.
Illustrations copyright © 1993 by K. Dyble Thompson.
"The Candles of Hanukkah" copyright © 1990 by Suni Paz (ASCAP).
All rights reserved. Published by Scholastic Inc., 555 Broadway, New York, NY
10012, by arrangement with Atheneum, Macmillan Publishing Company.
Designed by Kimberly M. Adlerman.
Printed in the U.S.A.
ISBN 0-590-48980-1

4  5  6  7  8  9  10        40        01  00  99

# Contents

1  On the Way to School                           1

2  Names and Surnames                             7

3  Recess                                        13

4  Mary López                                    18

5  The First Snowfall                            28

6  Thanksgiving                                  32

7  The Winter Pageant                            38

8  Trapped in a Spider's Web                     43

9  My Greatest Wish                              47

10 One Little Candle, Two Little Candles         53

# On the Way to School

María Isabel looked at the cup of coffee with milk and the buttered toast in front of her. But she couldn't bring herself to eat.

Her mother said, "Maribel, *cariño*, hurry up."

Her father added, "You don't want to be late on your first day, do you?"

But instead of finishing her breakfast, María Isabel just kept staring at the butter as it slowly melted into the toast, and at the cloud of steam that floated over her cup.

"You'll see, you'll like your new school," her mother said. But her mother's soft, reassuring voice didn't seem to convince María Isabel. María Isabel knew it wasn't going to be easy starting at a new school, especially when the school year had already begun. She was probably the only new student. She kept thinking what bad luck it was that they had had to move two months after school had started. And she had had so many plans to spend her winter vacation playing with Clara and Virginia.

"You'll make new friends soon," said María Isabel's father, as if he could read her thoughts.

María Isabel kept staring at the cup. But when her brother, Antonio, chimed in, "Come on, Belita, hurry up. You're going to make me late," she gulped down her coffee, even though it burned her tongue. María Isabel shook her head, trying to shake the nervous thoughts from her head.

She got up and grabbed her blue backpack. María Isabel had always wanted a backpack, and at the store last Saturday, this seemed to be just the right one. She had been so happy when her mother decided to buy it, even though it was more expensive than the red one. Later that day, when María Isabel was alone in the apartment, she had walked back and forth with the pack on her shoulders and had even climbed up onto the toilet seat to see how she looked in the bathroom mirror. But now it just seemed heavy, and María Isabel couldn't understand why she had liked it so much.

"Good-bye, Mami," María Isabel said softly to her mother, who was already washing the glasses and cups from breakfast.

"See you later, my love. May God be with you," her mother answered back, giving María Isabel a kiss on the forehead. Then she dunked her hands back into the soapy water.

"Good-bye, honey," her father said. "Be good at school and listen to your teacher. You know that your teacher at school is like your mother here at home."

"Yes, Papi. Good-bye," said María Isabel, and she got up on her tiptoes to hug her father. Then she took from the table the lunch bag her mother had prepared. María Isabel would have loved to stay in their warm kitchen with its smell of freshly brewed coffee. If only she could sit there all morning hugging her father, who always made her feel safe and secure. But a sudden blast of cold air told her that Antonio was waiting for her at the door.

By the time Antonio and María Isabel got to the front door of their apartment building, the yellow school bus was almost at the bus stop. "Come on, Belita. Run," Antonio called out.

María Isabel started to run. Her new boots, a present for her ninth birthday, made the dry leaves on the sidewalk crunch beneath her feet. In her rush to keep up with her brother, María Isabel did not see a section of sidewalk that was jutting up because of a tree root. Before she knew what had happened, she had tripped and fallen.

The first thing she heard was laughter. She didn't even realize that Antonio was talking to her. "Are you all right?" he asked her as he helped María Isabel off the ground.

María Isabel didn't answer him. She just bent down to pick up her smushed-up lunch bag. Her knee hurt a lot, but María Isabel was determined to walk to the bus without stopping to look at it. What she couldn't help but notice was the dress her mother had

washed and ironed so carefully the night before, and that was now streaked with dirt.

It was her favorite yellow dress, the dress that Aunt Aurea had made especially for her. María Isabel's grandmother had given her the fabric as a gift the last time they had gone to Puerto Rico to visit. María Isabel only wore the dress for special occasions. She had decided to wear it today for good luck on her first day of school. She had hoped the dress would help her feel a little less out of place with these new kids, the same new kids who were now laughing and chattering away on the bus while all María Isabel could do was look down at her bloody knee.

# Names and Surnames

"**G**ood morning," whispered María Isabel, standing in front of her new teacher's desk. Antonio had gone with her to the principal's office and then left to go to his own school, which was a block away. The secretary had given María Isabel a pink slip and then asked a boy to show her where Room 17 was. And now that she was there, María Isabel didn't know what would happen next.

The other kids had already taken their seats. Some were taking out their books and binders while others just seemed to be waiting for class to start. Many of them were smiling and talking to each other.

María Isabel looked up at an enormous turkey made of construction paper on the wall behind the teacher's desk. She started to read the names that were on each of the tail feathers: Jonathan, Eric, Michelle, Solomon, Laurie, Freddie, Marta, Ricardo, María Sánchez . . .

The teacher had not looked up yet. She was making notes in a large folder where María Isabel could see a list of names. María Isabel heard quiet laughter behind her. The teacher looked up only when the noise got louder.

"Why, hello," she said, giving María Isabel a warm smile. But it didn't seem to make María Isabel feel more comfortable. "So you are . . ."

"María Isabel Salazar López," she replied. In Spanish she would have added, "para servirle," but she didn't know how to say that in English. So María Isabel kept quiet and handed the pink slip to her teacher.

"Ah, María Lopez," the teacher said as she read the card. "We already have two Marías in this class. Why don't we call you Mary instead? Take a seat over there by Marta Pérez, and I'll give you your books later."

María Isabel quietly headed for her seat. Marta Pérez looked up from her book as María

Isabel came toward her. She had short hair and bangs. María Isabel lowered her eyes, and neither girl said a word.

A little while later, the teacher came over holding a thick book with a green cover. The book was brand-new and had a picture of a dolphin on the front. María Isabel wondered what the book was about, and if she would be able to read it. She loved the sea and had always dreamed of seeing a real dolphin, so she opened the book eagerly. On the inside cover the teacher had written the name Mary Lopez.

María Isabel stared at the words. Her teacher's handwriting was so neat and pretty. It seemed almost impossible to María Isabel that anyone could write so beautifully. As she looked at that strange name, Mary Lopez, María Isabel thought about her old schoolbooks. She had always enjoyed looking at the first page of a new book. Her mother's handwriting wasn't as pretty as her teacher's. But as they both sat at the kitchen table, her mother would write María Isabel's name in her new books, saying " 'María' is for your grandmother María, who you never knew but would have loved you so; 'Isabel' is for your grandmother Chabela, who loves you so dearly; 'Salazar' is for your father and, of course, for your grandfather Antonio; 'López' is for me and for your grandfather Manuel. You were very small when he died, but you would have loved him. Oh, the stories he would tell!"

María Isabel was proud of being named after her two grandmothers. Grandmother María was only a name to her, but she had often gazed at the picture that her father kept and cherished. Each time they moved, it was always the last thing to be packed, wrapped up neatly so it wouldn't get damaged. Later it would always be the first thing to be hung up on the wall of their new apartment.

And she liked being named after her grandmother Chabela, her sweet, smiling grandmother who lived in Puerto Rico and always seemed to smell of camomile, anisette, and cinnamon. Her sweets were so tasty that everyone would come by and try some. Grandmother Chabela kept the money she made selling her sweets in a tin cookie jar, and would tell María Isabel, "This is so you can study someday, my child, and not spend your

PUERTO RICO

whole life in a kitchen." She was the same Grandmother Chabela who had given her the fabric for the dress she was wearing, now streaked with blood and dirt.

"Mary. Mary Lopez. Mary *Lopeeez*," her teacher called out, her voice rising higher and higher. María Isabel's thoughts vanished like a puff of smoke. But it wasn't her teacher's shrill voice that shook her out of her daydreams but the silence that had followed in its wake.

"I'm talking to you, Mary." The teacher was now right by her desk, looking at María Isabel with a mix of surprise and impatience. María Isabel slumped down in her seat and looked at the dolphin that leaped across the cover of her book. She didn't know how to tell the teacher that she just didn't recognize herself in that strange new name.

# Recess

When the bell rang for recess, María Isabel waited for the rest of the kids to leave the class first. She wanted to see what they were going to do. María Isabel had started school in Puerto Rico. Then, when her family moved to the mainland, she had started going to another school. Her classes there had been in Spanish, and María Isabel had liked her teachers very much. Miss Herrera, who taught second grade, always praised her for her math, and she had started to teach María Isabel English. María Isabel especially liked Miss Peyrellade, her third grade teacher, who read wonderful stories and would teach the class outdoors on warm, sunny days.

María Isabel missed her old friends. She

didn't know anyone at this new school yet. So she just walked behind the other kids until they reached the schoolyard, and stood in a corner once she got there. After a few minutes, Marta Pérez came over and took her by the hand.

"Come on, let's go jump rope," Marta said, tugging on María Isabel's arm. María Isabel hesitated, and Marta tugged again. "Come on," she urged.

María Isabel followed Marta to the middle of the yard where she held one end of the jump rope as a girl in plaid jumped up and down. The rhythm of the jump rope as it brushed the ground was soothing. It reminded María Isabel of her grandmother Chabela's rocking chair, the one her grandmother would rock her to sleep in, or of the ebb and flow of the waves in front of her grandfather Antonio's house. The waves would gently roll up the beach in the small bay and wash over the sand where the fishing nets were drying on top of the boats.

María Isabel loved that beach. She loved to go out for a walk early in the morning, picking up treasures the sea had left behind the night

before: shells that looked like mother-of-pearl; bits of white coral; maybe even a sand dollar or two. And she liked to go swimming at midday, jumping in the waves and playing with the sea spray, feeling the coolness of the clear water beneath the hot sun.

"Go on, it's your turn," the girl in plaid shouted to María Isabel, bringing her back from her daydream.

"No, no," she answered in a low voice. "Not now." María Isabel didn't want the other girls to think she didn't know how to jump rope, but her knee still hurt from her fall. The girl in plaid jumped into the middle again. María Isabel thought, It would be so great to get in the middle and let the rope go back and forth, over and under me. My feet wouldn't touch the rope even once. But she didn't think she would be able to jump well with her hurt knee, and soon the bell rang. Recess was over.

María Isabel followed the two other girls. They hadn't spoken much, and she didn't know the name of the girl in plaid. But they had asked her to jump with them. Tomorrow, when her knee didn't hurt so much, she would show them how well she could jump. And as she limped slightly back to class, María Isabel thought this new school wasn't going to be so bad after all. If only her teacher would not insist on calling her Mary!

# Mary López

The next day, María Isabel found out that the girl in the plaid dress was one of the Marías in the class, María Fernández. The other María, María Sánchez, had very long braids and spent all her time at recess with her older sister.

María Isabel, on the other hand, began spending recess with María Fernández and Marta Pérez. She even jumped rope when they asked her to, even though her knee still hurt a little.

Over the next few days, she also got used to the rhythm of the school day. There was reading and math in the morning. Their teacher stressed doing well in math, and this was fine with María Isabel. She never had a problem working with numbers.

But best of all, Marta Pérez came up to her during lunch one day and said, "Come with me. I'll show you where the library is. They have tons of magazines!"

"Can we go without the teacher?" asked María Isabel.

"Sure. We can go in whenever we want to at lunchtime," replied Marta, pointing at an open door down the hall.

"Great!" said María Isabel. "At my other school, we could only go to the library when the teacher took the class."

The librarian was sitting at her desk behind some piles of books. She looked up as the girls came in, and smiled warmly. María Isabel felt that her smile was an invitation to feel at home.

Marta went straight to the magazines and grabbed a pile. She sat down on the rug, crossed her legs, and started to read a Batman comic.

María Isabel wandered between the stacks of books. She had never been left alone with so many books before, and she wasn't sure which one to pick. She looked at the titles carefully. Every now and then, she took a book off the shelf to look at the cover. She was holding a book in her hand when she realized the librarian was standing right next to her. María Isabel was surprised because she had not heard the librarian walk up to her, but she felt at ease looking into the woman's sparkling eyes. The librarian bent down and said quietly, as if she and María Isabel were sharing a secret, "Take it. You'll really like it."

As she walked out of the library, María Isabel thought, This new school really isn't so bad. It isn't so hard having classes only in English, and Marta Pérez is really nice. It's too bad Virginia and Clara aren't here, though.

But María Isabel's teacher lost her patience again that afternoon. The teacher asked if anyone knew who the Pilgrims were. Eric said they were sailors who had made a very long trip. Then the teacher turned to María Isabel and said, "Would Mary López tell us what she knows about the Pilgrims?"

María Isabel didn't answer. Again she didn't realize the teacher was calling on her. If she

had known, she would have said that the Pilgrims had come to America looking for a better way of life, and that many others came here after them. Perhaps she would even have dared to say that everyone was a Pilgrim in some way. That was what Miss Peyrellade had said.

But María Isabel didn't say anything, and her teacher was getting angry. She glared at María Isabel and said, "When I ask you something, you have to answer, Mary." She turned away and nodded at Solomon, who had raised his hand.

"The Pilgrims came to America to have freedom to practice their religion," Solomon answered.

María Isabel hung her head low for the rest of the afternoon. She worried that all the other kids would think that she was dumb for not having answered the teacher's question. The next day, she had trouble eating her breakfast again, and Antonio was annoyed with her.

"I don't want to have to run to the bus today, Belita," he complained. "Make her hurry, Mamá. Doesn't she care if she's late for school?"

Her mother didn't pay attention to Antonio, but she did help María Isabel put on her jacket and gave her her backpack and lunch bag.

While they were having a snack that afternoon, María Isabel's mother finally asked, "How was school today, Maribel?"

María Isabel said, "Fine." She didn't know what else to say. She felt she couldn't tell her mother that her math class was going well, but that she had forgotten to answer when her teacher called her Mary again that afternoon. And her teacher always seemed to be upset with her.

Antonio, on the other hand, couldn't stop talking about his new friends and about the great band his school had. Or about the baseball team. But even though Antonio talked on and on, their mother didn't really seem to listen. She seemed to have a lot on her mind lately.

The family had moved because Mr. Salazar had a new job cleaning and maintaining a small group of apartment buildings. And as a part of the job, his family could live in one of the apartments. María Isabel's parents had been happy about the move because now they wouldn't have to pay rent anymore. Antonio was happy because the apartment had three bedrooms, and he would finally have a room of his own. And Antonio always liked new things.

But Mrs. Salazar was having trouble getting used to the new neighborhood. She couldn't find the ingredients she used in her cooking. She would try to substitute new things, but she wasn't happy with the results. And even though they didn't have to pay rent for the apartment, Mr. Salazar's pay didn't seem to go far enough to make ends meet.

At dinner that night, Mrs. Salazar announced, "I'm going to look for a job tomorrow. I'll try to be home when you children get home from school, but here is a key to the door in case I'm not." María Isabel's mother handed her a key attached to a long pink ribbon. "Come straight home from school and wait for me here. Don't leave the house, and don't open the door to anyone."

María Isabel felt a little strange the next day, walking around with the pink ribbon around her neck. In one way, it wasn't that unusual. She had always worn something around her neck. First, it had been a pendant with the image of the Virgin Mary, a baptism present from her godmother. Then she had worn a cross that her godfather had given her when she was seven years old. María Isabel was so used to wearing something around her neck that she usually forgot it was there. But the key was different. At times, it made her feel important and grown up. María Isabel noticed that some of the other girls also wore keys, and she felt that they all had something in common. Most of the day, though, the key just made her feel sad.

When she finally got home and opened the door, all María Isabel found was silence. Her mother wasn't there. Antonio had stayed after school for band practice. Ever since he learned to play the drums, Antonio spent all his free time practicing.

The apartment felt like an empty box. María Isabel sat down at the kitchen table. She took out a piece of paper and a pencil from her backpack and started to write: *María Isabel Salazar López, María Isabel Salazar López, María Isabel Salazar López*. Each time she wrote her name, the letters got bigger and bigger until she reached the bottom of the page. María Isabel crumpled the paper up into a ball and threw it at the garbage can, but she missed. She thought about how Antonio would tease her about her aim if he were here and, for a moment, she was glad to be alone. She got up and put the crumpled page in the trash. Then she went to see what there was to eat in the kitchen cabinet.

María Isabel had set the table by the time her father got home from work. Dinner was almost ready. A large bowl of salad sat in the center of the table, while the rice and beans on the stove top were ready to be served. The only thing left to do was to cook the meat.

Mrs. Salazar was exhausted when she got home. She plopped down into a chair and took off her shoes. She smiled when she saw the food and the table.

After they had all sat down to eat, father said, "You've done a wonderful job of helping your mother, María Isabel."

Her mother quickly added, "The rice is delicious! We did the right thing naming you María Isabel. You are as good a cook as your grandmother Chabela."

Antonio didn't say anything, but he did help himself to more beans.

María Isabel wanted to smile and be happy. She liked pleasing her parents, and she knew she had done a good job making dinner. But the same thought kept running through her head, over and over again: How can I feel proud of being named María Isabel when I have to listen so carefully every time the teacher calls for "Mary Lopez"?

# The First Snowfall

The city was covered by a beautiful blanket of snow. María Isabel couldn't tear herself away from her bedroom window. The snow had covered up all the trash cans and had turned the alleyway her room faced into an enchanted tunnel. The city seemed to be wrapped in silence.

María Isabel tried to step in Antonio's boot prints as they walked to the bus stop. She didn't want to do anything to disturb the wonderful, newly fallen snow. Once she was at school, she kept thinking about the snow all during math. María Isabel wondered if there was enough snow in the alleyway to make a snowman, and if she would be able to see it from her window.

Suddenly she remembered that she hadn't finished her multiplication exercises, and hurried to complete her work. María Isabel was so busy trying to finish the page that she didn't hear the teacher call out, in an irritated tone of voice, "Mary Lopez!" When at last she realized that the teacher was waiting for an answer from her, María Isabel had no idea what the question had been.

"Well, it looks like Mary doesn't want to take part in our Winter Pageant," the teacher said. "That's all right. You can help Tony and Jonathan greet the parents at the door and show them where they can put the food and hang up their coats."

The Winter Pageant . . . María Isabel couldn't think about anything else on the ride home from school. The teacher had told them they would be staging *Amahl and the Night Visitors*. María Isabel remembered seeing the story on television once and liking it very much. I know I wouldn't have gotten to play Mary, she thought, because Ann would be so much better for that part, with her long hair and all. But I would have loved to be a shepherd. I could have used Mama's straw basket, and it would have been so wonderful. . . .

María Isabel turned toward the window of the school bus so that no one would see her wiping a tear. When she looked out, she saw that the morning's bright, clean snow had been shoveled and trampled, and was now covered with soot and grime. She wished that she could be with her friend Clara. Clara would understand how María Isabel felt.

María Isabel took out her library book and started to read. She didn't want to look at the dirty snow or think about the pageant anymore. The book was titled *Charlotte's Web*. Fern's life on the farm seemed so simple and carefree to María Isabel. She would have liked to live that way, surrounded by farm animals. She would have plenty of time to sit in the barn and listen to them talk. María Isabel wondered, Why can't real life be more like the books I read?

SCH

# Thanksgiving

On Thanksgiving Day, Mr. and Mrs. Salazar decided to visit their friends in the old neighborhood. It was a last-minute decision they made after dinner was over, when it felt to everyone that there was something missing. The Salazar family had known a lot of people in their old apartment building, and there was always someone to say hello to or to invite in for some coffee and conversation.

Antonio and María Isabel were delighted. On the long subway ride, María Isabel thought about all the things she'd tell Clara and Virginia about her new school.

As soon as they got to the Hernández apartment, María Isabel asked if she could go and visit her friends. She ran upstairs to the third floor to Virginia's apartment. Her next-door neighbor said Virginia had gone to have Thanksgiving dinner at her grandparents'. So María Isabel went to see if Clara was home. When Clara opened the door, her face broke into a big smile, and she hugged María Isabel. María Isabel thought Clara had changed a lot. Then she realized that her friend was wearing makeup. Clara wanted María Isabel to meet her cousin who lived next door. She had just arrived from Puerto Rico.

"Her name is Carmen. And she's thirteen! I know you'll like her," Clara said as she rang the doorbell.

Carmen answered the door. "What a pretty friend you have!" she exclaimed as she led the two girls into the apartment. She looked at María Isabel and added, "Come with me. I'll make you even prettier."

Carmen went into her room and came back with a plastic box full of makeup. She sat María Isabel down in front of a mirror and started to work on her face. Carmen painted María Isabel's lips, put some blush on her cheeks, and applied some eye shadow. Then she brushed María Isabel's hair back and pinned it with a flowered barrette.

"Carmen is going to be a hairdresser," said Clara. "Isn't she good?"

"And a makeup artist," Carmen added. "Someday I'm going to work in Hollywood and do the makeup for all the big stars."

"And you'll know them all!" Clara said excitedly.

Carmen went back into her room to get some magazines. She told the girls all sorts of things about the movie stars in the magazines, and about how she would make up each one.

An hour had gone by before María Isabel knew it. "I have to wash my face," she said. "My mother doesn't want me to wear makeup yet."

"No, don't wash your face," said Carmen. "I'll take most of it off with a tissue." Carmen wiped off the makeup, leaving only a trace behind. María Isabel got up to leave.

"Wait, don't go yet," Carmen said, and she dabbed some perfume on María Isabel's wrists.

"Thanks a lot, Carmen. I hope I'll see you again before you go to Hollywood." Clara

walked María Isabel back to the Hernández apartment. They walked slowly, trying to stretch their remaining time together.

"How come you never call me? Or Virginia either?" Clara finally asked her.

"Mamá doesn't want us to use the phone unless we have to. But I'll ask if I can call you Sunday," she replied.

"And I'll call you on the Sunday after that," Clara said as they reached the Hernándezes' door.

On the way home, María Isabel thought of all the things that she didn't tell Clara about her new school, especially about her teacher, who always seemed to be so angry with her. They'd had such a good time that she had forgotten all about school. She was already looking forward to calling Clara on Sunday. María Isabel was smiling quietly to herself when suddenly Antonio said, "It looks like your friends think it's Carnaval instead of Thanksgiving."

María Isabel tried to bury her face in her coat. She should have washed her face after all. But her father just laughed. "Leave your sister alone, Antonio. Chabelita is going to be a very pretty young woman someday."

Mr. Salazar leaned over and hugged his daughter. "But that day hasn't come yet. Right, Chabelita?"

María Isabel saw that her mother was smiling too, and then she knew that there really were good reasons to be thankful on this Thanksgiving.

# The Winter Pageant

Everything at school now revolved around plans for the Winter Pageant. The class was making wreaths and lanterns. The teacher explained to the class that Christmas is celebrated differently in different countries, and that many people don't celebrate Christmas at all. They talked about Santa Claus, and how he is called Saint Nicholas in some countries and Father Christmas in others. The class also talked about the Jewish feast of Hanukkah that celebrates the rededication of the Temple of Jerusalem, and about the special meaning of the nine candles of the Hanukkah menorah.

The teacher had asked everyone to bring in pictures or other things having to do with the holidays. A lot of kids brought in photographs of their families by their Christmas trees. Mayra brought in pictures of New Year's Day in Santo Domingo. Michelle brought in a picture of herself sitting on Santa's lap when she was little. Gabriel brought in photos of the Three Kings' Day parade in Miami, Florida. He had been there last year, when he went to visit his Cuban grandmother. Marcos brought in a piñata shaped like a green parrot that his uncle had brought back from Mexico. Emmanuel showed everyone a photo album of his family's trip to Israel, and Esther brought in cards her grandfather had sent her from Jerusalem.

One day, Suni Paz came to the school. She sang Christmas songs from different countries and taught the class to sing a Hanukkah song, "The Candles of Hanukkah."

María Isabel went home humming softly "Hanukkah . . . Hanukkah . . . Let us celebrate." The bus trip seemed a lot shorter as the song ran through her head. It almost felt as if she had traveled to all those different countries and had celebrated all those different holidays.

María Isabel was still singing while she made dinner and set the table:

"With our menorah,
Fine potato latkes,
Our clay trumpets,
Let us celebrate."

Her voice filled the empty kitchen. María Isabel was so pleased she promised herself that she'd make a snowman the next time it snowed. And she'd get it finished before the garbage men picked up the trash and dirtied up the snow.

But after Suni Paz's visit to the school, the days seemed to drag by more and more slowly. María Isabel didn't have anything to do during rehearsals, since she didn't have a part in *Amahl.*

The teacher decided that after the play the actors would sing some holiday songs, including María Isabel's favorite about the Hanukkah candles. Since she didn't have a part, María Isabel wouldn't be asked to sing either.

It didn't seem to matter much to Tony and Jonathan, the other two kids who weren't in

the play. They spent rehearsal time reading comics or whispering to each other. Neither boy spoke to María Isabel, and she was too shy to say anything to them.

The only fun she had was reading her library book. Somehow her problems seemed so small compared to Wilbur the pig's. He was in danger of becoming the holiday dinner. María Isabel felt the only difference was that the characters in books always seemed to find answers to their problems, while she couldn't figure out what to do about her own.

As she cut out bells and stars for decorations, María Isabel daydreamed about being a famous singer. Someday she would sing in front of a large audience, and her teacher would feel guilty that she had not let María Isabel sing in the Winter Pageant.

But later María Isabel thought, My teacher isn't so bad. It's all a big misunderstanding. . . . If only there was some way I could let her know. Even if I'm not a great singer someday, it doesn't matter. All I really want is to be myself and not make the teacher angry all the time. I just want to be in the play and to be called María Isabel Salazar López.

# Trapped in a Spider's Web

"I've asked my boss if I can leave work early the day of the school pageant," María Isabel's mother said one evening as she served the soup. "Papá is also going to leave work early. That way we'll be able to bring the rice and beans."

"And best of all, we can hear María Isabel sing," her father added.

María Isabel looked down at her soup. She had not told her parents anything. She knew they were going to be very disappointed when they saw the other kids in her class taking part in the play. She could just hear her mother asking, "Why didn't you sing? Doesn't the teacher know what a lovely voice you have?"

María Isabel ate her soup in silence. What could she say?

"Don't you have anything to say, Chabelita?" asked her father. "Aren't you glad we're coming?"

"Sure, Papá, sure I am," said María Isabel, and she got up to take her empty bowl to the sink.

After helping her mother with the dishes, María Isabel went straight to her room. She put on her pajamas and got into bed. But she couldn't sleep, so she turned the light on and continued reading *Charlotte's Web*. María Isabel felt that she was caught in a sticky, troublesome spider's web of her own, and the more she tried to break loose, the more trapped she became.

When the librarian had told her that she would like the book, María Isabel had felt that they were sharing a secret. Now as she turned the pages, she thought that maybe the secret was that *everyone* has problems. She felt close to poor little Wilbur, being fattened up for Christmas dinner without even knowing it. He was a little like her parents, who were so

eager to go to the pageant, not knowing what was waiting for them.

"It just isn't fair that this can't be a happy time for all of us!" María Isabel said out loud. She sighed. Then she turned off the light, snuggled under her blanket, and fell asleep trying to figure out a way to save Wilbur from becoming Christmas dinner.

# 9

# My Greatest Wish

Two days were left until the pageant. The morning was cloudy and gray. On the way to school, María Isabel wondered if it was going to snow. Maybe she would be able to make that snowman. But shortly after she got to school, it started to drizzle.

Since they couldn't go outside, the students spent their time rehearsing. No one made a mistake. Melchior didn't forget what he had to say to Amahl's mother. Amahl dropped his crutch only once. Best of all, though, the shepherds remembered when they were supposed to enter, without bumping into the Three Kings.

Even Tony and Jonathan seemed interested in the play. They volunteered to help carry the manger and the shepherds' baskets on- and offstage.

Satisfied with the final rehearsal, the teacher decided there was time for one last class exercise before vacation. "It's been a couple of days since we've done some writing," she said when the students returned to class. "The new year is a time for wishes. Sometimes wishes come true; sometimes they don't. But it's important to have wishes and, most of all, to know what you really want. I'd like you all to take out some paper and write an essay titled 'My Greatest Wish.' "

María Isabel sighed and put away *Charlotte's Web*. Charlotte had just died, and María Isabel wondered what was going to happen to the sack of eggs that Wilbur had saved, and when Charlotte's babies would be born. But María Isabel would have to wait to find out. She bit down on her pencil and wrote: "My greatest wish . . ."

This shouldn't be so hard, María Isabel thought. If I finish writing early, I can probably finish my book. She started to write: "My greatest wish is to make a snowman. . . ."

María Isabel read over what she had just

written, and realized that it wasn't what she really wanted. She put the paper aside, took out a new sheet, and wrote down the title again. "My greatest wish is to have a part in *Amahl.* . . ."

María Isabel stopped writing again. She thought, Would Charlotte have said that her greatest wish was to save Wilbur? Or would she have wished for something impossible, like living until the next spring and getting to know her children? The teacher just said that wishes don't always come true. If I'm going to wish for something, it should be something really worth wishing for.

María Isabel took out a third sheet of paper and wrote down the title again. This time, she didn't stop writing until she got to the bottom of the page.

### My Greatest Wish

*When I started to write I thought my greatest wish was to make a snowman. Then I thought my greatest wish was to have a part in the Winter Pageant. But I think my greatest wish is to be called*

*María Isabel Salazar López. When that was my name, I felt proud of being named María like my papá's mother, and Isabel, like my grandmother Chabela. She is saving money so that I can study and not have to spend my whole life in a kitchen like her. I was Salazar like my papá and my grandpa Antonio, and López, like my grandfather Manuel. I never knew him but he could really tell stories. I know because my mother told me.*

*If I was called María Isabel Salazar López, I could listen better in class because it's easier to hear than Mary López. Then I could have said that I wanted a part in the play. And when the rest of the kids sing, my mother and father wouldn't have to ask me why I didn't sing, even though I like the song about the Hanukkah candles so much.*

The rest of the class had already handed in their essays and were cleaning out their desks to go home when María Isabel got up. She quietly went to the front of the room and put her essay on the teacher's desk. María Isabel didn't look up at the teacher, so she didn't see the woman smiling at her. She hurried back to her desk to get her things and leave.

# 10

# One Little Candle,
# Two Little Candles

Holiday spirit was everywhere at school the next day. The paper wreaths and lanterns the class had made were hung up all over the room. The teacher had put the "greatest wish" essays up on the bulletin board, next to the cutouts of Santa Claus, the Three Kings, and a menorah.

All the students were restless. Marta Pérez smiled when María Isabel sat down next to her. "Look at the pretty Christmas card I got from my cousin in Santo Domingo," she said excitedly. María Isabel looked at the tropical Christmas scene, all trimmed in flowers. But she couldn't answer Marta because the teacher had started to speak.

"We're going to do one last rehearsal because there's a small change in the program."

The rest of the kids listened attentively, but María Isabel just kept looking down at her desk. After all, she had nothing to do with the pageant.

Then she heard the teacher say, "María Isabel, María Isabel Salazar López . . ." María Isabel looked up in amazement.

"Wouldn't you like to lead the song about the Hanukkah candles?" the teacher said with a wide grin. "Why don't you start by yourself, and then everyone else can join in. Go ahead and start when you're ready."

María Isabel walked nervously up to the front of the room and stood next to the teacher, who was strumming her guitar. Then she took a deep breath and began to sing her favorite holiday song.

While her mother was getting the rice and beans ready that night, Mr. Salazar called María Isabel over to him. "Since you can't wear makeup yet, Chabelita, I've brought you something else that I think you'll like." In the palm of his hand were two barrettes for her hair. They were shaped like butterflies and gleamed with tiny stones.

"Oh, Papi. They're so pretty! Thank you!" María Isabel exclaimed. She hugged her father and ran to her room to put them on.

At school the next day, María Isabel stood in the center of the stage. She was wearing her special yellow dress, a pair of new shoes, and the shining butterflies. She spoke clearly to the audience. "My name is María Isabel Salazar López. I'm going to sing a song about the Jewish feast of Hanukkah, that celebrates the rededication of the Temple in Jerusalem." The music started, and María Isabel began to sing:

The Candles of Hanukkah

One little candle,
Two little candles,
Three little candles,
Let us celebrate.
Four little candles,
Five little candles,
Six little candles,
Let us celebrate.

Hanukkah, Hanukkah,
Let us celebrate.
    Seven little candles,
    Eight little candles,
    Nine little candles,
    Let us celebrate.
Hanukkah, Hanukkah,
Let us celebrate.
    With our menorah,
    Fine potato latkes,
    Our clay trumpets,
    Let us celebrate.
    With our family,
    With our friends,
    With our presents,
    Let us celebrate.

And the butterflies in María Isabel's hair sparkled under the stage lights so much that it seemed that they might just take off and fly.